Copyrighted 2022
© TalleyMarks Publishing LLC
Author: Stephen J. Talley

All rights reserved. No part of this publication may be reproduced, distributed, or transmitted in any form or by any means, including photocopying, recording, or other electronic or mechanical methods, without the prior written permission of the publisher, except in the case of brief quotations embodied in critical reviews and certain other non-commercial uses permitted by copyright law.

This is a work of fiction. Names, characters, businesses, places, events and incidents are either the products of the author's imagination or used in a fictitious manner. Any resemblance to actual persons, living or dead, or actual events is coincidental.

Table of Contents

1. Fool's Gold
2. A Golden Lesson "Sex Heals Nothing"
3. Just Another Day
4. Lil O
5. Golden GoodNights
6. A Golden Vision
7. Golden Light Reveals
8. Golden Instincts
9. Golden Acceptance
10. The Golden Crown Of A Queen
11. A Golden Hit
12. Golden Beginnings and Painful Endings
13. A Golden Cry
14. Golden Code
15. A Golden Partnership
16. Golden Words Upon Paper
17. My Golden Queen (Teresa)
18. My Golden Creation (Marie Monet)

Fool's Gold

She knows it, damn,
I was caught within her web,
Her walk, her smile,
Those curves, those eyes,
Why would I do this to myself,
I shouldn't be here but I am,
I know better,
But me knowing better is what's
driving me crazy,
Look at her,
So sure she has me,
As if she was listening to me think,
With a devilish smirk on her face,
She asked, " what are you thinking about?"
Too quickly I replied, " nothing! "
Giving away the truth,
My bluff was as weak as my actions,
As I stated before,
I was caught in her web,

Like a spider she could feel all
vibes within her domain,
She licked her lips,
Walked towards me,
Naturally seductive,
Her aroma made my manhood jump,
Those hazel almond eyes,
Could see straight through me,
I was so fucking wrong,
She was supposed to be off limits,
But she reminded me of someone,
Laura Winslow!
Yep, the one from Family Matters,
Looking at her in that moment,
That's exactly what I was thinking,
Even crazier than that,
As her eyes attached themselves to the rising bulge between my legs,

Jokingly, but again as if she was in my head,
She asked, " Did I do that? "
I didn't respond with words,
I just smirked and giggled lightly,
My morals left with my blood,
My big head was now being deprived,
It was no longer in control,
My little head had taken the wheel,
My heart fought to free me,
I began to see her,
I couldn't stop thinking of the negative consequences,
She was thinking of me,
I always knew when she did,
But she understood our connection much deeper than me,
She always knew when I was fucking up,

And I was fucking up bad,
Just as I thought of leaving,
I felt my pants and draws leave my
waistline instead,
Before I could react,
Truthfully I don't think much would
have changed even if I could've,
Stacey was licking the tip
of my manhood,
Then she devoured me,
Well she attempted too,
But she began gagging,
As if my hands were around her throat,
The gagging created the wetness I needed,
She was sucking this dick like she loved it,
She was eating this dick like a pro,

Slurping, licking, and encouraging me
to fuck her throat,
She spit on my dick,
Then began stroking it,
While she filled her mouth with my balls,
She moaned lightly,
Her juices had soaked her panties,
She was pleasuring herself from pleasing me,
Her satisfaction was my bodies reaction,
Her effort shifted gears,
As I palmed the back of her head,
Then aggressively fucked her mouth,
While talking my shit,
Reality hit,
I could feel my phone vibrating
on my ankle,

Thoughts of my infidelity,
Were at level fuck it,
This was her friend,
Somebody she loved,
I had fallen weak,
Teresa didn't deserve this,
Stacey looked me in the eyes,
Then pop my manhood out of her mouth,
She knew what I was thinking,
She could feel the vibrations too,
While licking my stiffness,
She found the words to form the question,
"Are you going to answer it?",
I didn't find the words to answer back,
I just licked my thumb,
Wetting it with my middle

and index finger with it,
I began massage her beautiful full
brown nipples,
That were stood erect upon the perfection
that were her breast,
34C, and they were hers,
No work created by a surgeon,
Could have created this woman,
She was the creation of The Creator,
But her beauty was shallow,
Her actions now,
Only proved she hated herself,
Just like me,
Unaware of what's to be loved
about who I was,
So we hurt others,
Like vampires, but for energy,
But we were the same,

I'd gone too far anyway,
But I'd planned to go much further,
Starting now, as I slide my middle finger
into her asshole,
She moaned in way that let me know,
She loved it,
And even greater than anything else,
She was H^2O,
There was no scent at all,
No perfume or cover up,
Just a petite bubble butt,
Chocolate covered,
And pretty pussy,
Waxed, not shaved,
I slapped her ass,
Leaving my handprint imprinted
on her ass,
I wanted to,

But I wasn't going to,
Then again,
Fuck it, naw I don't eat pussy,
I suck it,
I french kiss it,
Take my time savoring the taste,
Vrrmmm... vrrmmm,
Again and again my phone rang,
But Stacey was fucking my face,
I felt her cum,
Then I tasted her, she quivered,
Then moaned in a panting type of way,
She exploded,
I stuck my tongue deep in her,
The juices wouldn't be wasted,
To further fuck her up,
I applied more pressure,
I slid my thumb in her ass,
And locked her hands to her feet,

Holding her wrist to her ankles,
I was relentlessly stuffing my face,
She relentlessly tried to escape,
But was clamped in place,
I told her to beg,
She moaned deeply, " pleaseeeeeee T!"
I released her,
But I was far from done,
Her fountain of youth was talking,
She had no idea of the snake that was stalking,
Her eyes were closed,
She was still breathing deep,
That too was taken away,
As my girth and full extent of my length,
Slowly slid into her soul,
Missionary is how we began,

With every thrust of my gyrating hips,
She felt me in her stomach,
Beating her box up,
Jabbing her deeply,
I flipped her over,
She was positioned like a bitch,
And I was a big dog,
My balls smacked her clit,
Each time I dug deep,
I knocking layers loss like a shovel,
As if I was preparing for a burial,
Because I was killing that pussy,
As she released all over my meat,
She asked me to stretch her other hole,
She spread her cheeks,
Again begging,
She stated seductively

," please take it slow!",
I spit on it,
Then I massaged it with 2 fingers,
I prepared her properly,
Before I entered slowly,
Gradually I picked up the pace,
Shortly after,
She had become a daycare,
As I spilled potential seeds into her hole,
When I pulled out
She put my dick back in her mouth,
She'd been waiting on this moment,
My toes were curled,
As attempted to again take my soul,
I was the one now attempting to run,
But when I did,
She tightly squeezed my balls,
On life she fucked me up,

Eating up all my nut,
Then cleaning me up,
She knew I needed to go,
I had no time to chill,
47 missed calls,
We'd be at it for 2hrs,
I was home before I answered the phone,
Teresa didn't get off work until 6am,
It was 3am when I picked up the phone,
On her 48th attempt,
Hello…….

A Golden Lesson

"Sex Heals Nothing"

I pick up the phone,
Knowing I was wrong,
She didn't even let me say hello,
She went straight into combat mode,
You fucking hoe,
I could feel the tears in her voice,
I didn't want to lie,
But telling the truth was out
of the question at this point,
I had no choice but to lie,
I felt so heartless,
One lie becomes an oceanic darkness so quick,
I was sleeping, Bae
A lie can only be supported by another lie,
A support system that's hollow and weak,
Quickly crumbling when tested by truth,
Yet able to stand beautifully,
Until that of the dark,
Finds its way to the light,
Dismantling its existence,
You lying ass hoe,
The venom in her words crippled my soul,
She was hurting,
And it was solely my fault,
Before I couldn't say anything else,

She came through the door,
Throwing her phone like Greg Maddox,
I ducked her enraged attack,
The phone just missed me,
The impact of its collision with the wall,
Guaranteed it was no longer operational,
She charged me,
Her feet crunching pieces of her phone
as she reached me,
Love had evolved into hatred,

I wasn't going to hit her back,
I was guilty,
What could I say,
We'd been together for years,
We were connected,
Me lying; in truth, was pointless,
One thing I could never hide,
Was the imbalance of my energy,
She was in tune and understood
those things,
Things I had not yet begun to understand,
What I did understand,
Was the energy in that smack,
It took at least 3 days from my life,
Teresa was small,
She was petite, 5'1"
Chocolate, the real chocolate,
She was brown,
Not black,
She was curvy,
Well she poked out in

all the right places,
128 pounds soaking wet,
With deep dimples in her cheeks,
A rounded face,
With cheekbones that were
structured perfectly,
The most beautiful white teeth,
Lie perfectly behind her full beautiful lips,
Her nose wasn't small,
But it wasn't big,
It was perfect,
I truly believed,
She was gorgeous,
But within this moment,
I had to calm her little ass down,
I grabbed her and held her tightly,
But the anger within her was boiling,
She would be felt,
One way or another,
She screamed, " I hate you bitch! ",
I looked her in the eyes,

Hurt filled them as I replied," you don't
mean that shit!?",
She was doing all she could to get free,
I tried kissing her forehead,
That was a mistake,
And an opportunity she did not waste,
Swiftly she head butted me,
" Let me go, bitch! " she yelled at the top
of her lungs,
She was like a rabid wolf,
Foam building in the corners of her mouth,
While my top lip was bleeding,
It took 20 minutes,
She had finally calmed down,
Crying uncontrollably,
Her tears flooded my arms
and dampened my shirt,
She asked me, " why?! "
I deflected the question,

" why what ? ",
Quickly lacing lies told,
With lies I had not yet expressed,
She asked,
No! She demanded, " let me see your phone! "
This is where I shift gears,
This is the point I would take back control,
I'm nobody's fool,
Nobody but, family had this number,
I relaxed and gave it straight to her,
But again, we're connected,
She felt the deceit,
I wasn't shit,
This was the worst thing I could ever
do as a man,
Insecurities will drive us both insane,
I was acting like a boy,
Not controlling myself,
Allowing my head without a brain,
To misguide my head that has one,

I couldn't stop lying,
I didn't want to lose her,
So I didn't speak,
I kissed her lips, well I tried to,
She turned her head,
As if I was,
What I actually was,
Unable to prove it,
But beyond ever being of categorized
with those considered to be stupid,
She snapped the words at me,
" Get the fuck off me! "
I knew she didn't want to mean it,
So I kissed her cheek,
Then her neck, and collarbone,
She tried pulling away,
But I pulled her back in,
Tightly embracing her,
I could tell this was what she truly wanted,
So I attempted to kiss her again,
This time she didn't pull back,

She didn't turn her head away,
She leaned in,
Meeting me halfway,
Deeply we kissed,
Passionately we spoke energetically,
My apologies were felt,
As her body trembled in anticipation,
Yes, she had just left work,
But bae wasn't an average hygiene type girl,
I wasted no time,
I bent her straight over the arm of the sofa,
She was already wet as fuck,
And I know better than to waste water,
So I sucked the juices off her pussy,
I kissed it, twirling my tongue around the clit,
But I had other plans,
And she couldn't wait,
Spreading her ass cheeks,

Simultaneously her pussy smacked softly,
Like wet lips do when they slowly part,
I spit in her asshole,
Then start my tongue's journey at the end of her spine,
I circle the hole,
I tease her, only dipping,
Then expanding a small portion of my lethal weapon,
I massaged her clit,
While I teased,
Then I entered her,
Fucking her with my tongue,
She cums,
Her juices run down the two fingers
I slid into her warmth,
She shakes as her pussy pulsates,
But I'm so far from done,
I pick her up,
Then lay her on her back,
Pull a chair up,

Then I smothered myself,
From my chin,
To my nose,
I know she was overwhelmed,
The pressure kept building,
Then releasing,
She was damn near out,
Damn near unable to talk,
In a pleading tone, but so sexy,
I couldn't stop,
Because I wanted to hear it again,
She said, " okkkkkk…. Ok bae please! "
But as I stated before,
I didn't let go until the second time she asked,
I had to get to the block,
Too much of my day had already been lost,
The sun hadn't even allowed the moon to rest,
And I was already way behind schedule,

A schedule that I myself had set,
So I didn't fuck,
Knowing I was already in need of energy,
I ran Teresa's shower water,
While she showered,
I cooked breakfast,
We ate and she went straight to bed,
I ate, then lined up the route I would take,
I had a nice check to accumulate,
So I got to work,
After telling Teresa,
I loved her,
We kissed, but before I left the room,
I heard her snore,
She was exhausted,
Physically and emotionally,
I had to do better,
She needed and deserved
the best of me,

So the best of me,
Is exactly what I plan to give!

Just Another Day

I'm knee deep in the game,
But on my own accord,
I handle my business,
I don't owe a soul,
Vibing through traffic,
In my drop head,
Trying to clear my mind,
Thug Motivation's Standing Ovation
was bumpin,
Jeezy got a young nigga through,
I swear the nigga knew my life,
My Mustang's engine growled,
As I floored the gas down i65,
Leaving Drentwood,
One of the upper ends of the Ville,
Bashville, my home,
The South Side,
Now partially gentrified,
But still a goldmine,
One that I've been mining my whole life,
I clocked in more hours than
a four year has lived,
I was far too seasoned,

Even at 19,
To be on the block and not
have my head in the game,
This wasn't the place to play,
But so many do,
So many become lost,
They lose themselves,
I promise,
I understand their struggle,
Because, we share it,
I'm no different from them
As you can see,
I can't keep my dick in my pants,
So clearly I'm not yet mature,
Growth is necessary,
I'm doing the best I can do,
Fuck it,
This is all I know,
I was raised without being raised,
How could I be something I've
never known,
I had to pull up on Lil O,
Lil O was my nigga One,

One wasn't his real name,
It was the tag I gave him,
Lil O was 18,
We grew up on the same team,
I'd known him my whole life,
I called him One,
Cause he was the only One
I trusted in these streets,
And even though he was younger
than me,
I'd never consider my brother
to be my underling,
We rocked on the same vibe,
We handled whatever,
Whenever,
I didn't even have to question if O
was riding,
10 times out of 10,
I was a 100% sure,
I had 8 under my feet,
O had like 5 of his own,
O stayed on the same block we grew up on,
But our hood had been gentrified,

He was one of the only originals,
But the neighborhood was still filled
with copper toned people,
Just not the type we grew around,
The hood was completely different,
In a good way,
O crib was 400k,
He didn't buy it cash,
But don't get it twisted,
The lil nigga was getting it,
That's why I was pulling up on him today,
I didn't deal with many,
As a matter of fact,
I didn't deal with anybody but O,
We had came a long way, The plug chose me 3 years ago,
When I was 16,
Before that, I was kickin in doors,
Nickel and dimin,
But I never accumulated a check,
Now I was signing them bitches,
As I got off the states,
And swung a left on Wedgewood,

I put my rag over glock 19 that was in my lap,
You never know what one time
would be ridin in,
But I always had my tool close,
With one in the head,
I pulled up,
Lil O was outside hooping,
Him and his lil brother,
O raised him,
Because like me,
O parents were gone,
But in a different way,
His moms smoked crack,
His dad went to the store
before he was even born,
The nigga never came back,
The hood was like that,
So many of us shared the same story,
So many of us grew up without any guidance,
At this point it's was an excuse,
That's how society viewed it,

Because society only spoke about the trenches,
From a bird's eye view,
As I stepped out my whip,
My phone binged 3 times,
I already knew it was home,
But I had to handle this business,
So I didn't even bother to look at it,
I had to count up this paper,
Plus we had other issues to discuss,
So we did,
This issue that we had to discuss,
Needed to be handled immediately,
So I put in the order,
Both of them,
For my next shipment,
And for these lil fleas,
Thinking my blocks could be shared,
It was plenty for us all,
True enough,
That wasn't the point at all,
Niggas reckless actions,
Can bring heat on us,

So examples needed to be made,
And I wasn't about to play,
Immediate response to the encroachment,
Whether or not they knew,
Didn't mean shit to me,
They should've did their homework,
This is business,
Location is everything,
And respect is even more vital,
So I thought it out while I was thinking,
I'll offer the niggas a job,
On some get down or lay down shit,
I had to think of how the violence would affect us,
Being a boss meant,
Making boss decisions,
So I put a hold on the hit,
I told O to check the niggas temperatures,
As I was walking out,
With a duffel bag of government issued IOU's,
My phone binged again,
But this time I viewed it,

It was Bae, like I thought,
But the shit it stated,
Had my feet locked,
O asked what's the word,
I told him, " Teresa's pregnant! ",
Happily O yelled, " oh word! ",
But that's not it fam,
O looked at me like spit then,
She told me she wasn't raising our child in this world of bullshit,
She gave me an ultimatum,
She said, " It's our family, or that game that's filled with games! "
O looked at me, knowing what I would choose,
We dapped up,
Expressed love like brothers do,
I needed to get home,
My choice was already made,
My days in this game were numbered,
It was time for me to put my exit plan in action!

Lil O

Big Bro told me to check their temp,
But he didn't know,
I couldn't tell him,
He had too much on his plate already,
So I didn't tell him,
But this would be a beautiful way
for my brother to end this chapter,
I knew he was serious,
So I knew what that meant for me,
I was prepared for that moment,
But this moment was right here in front of me,
These three bitches were on some double negative type shit,
Which meant a positive for me,
Slipping wasn't even the word,
Coming out of the club drunk,
On whatever the fuck else they were on,
They had know idea,
The ride the bartender offered wasn't an Uber,
These niggas were prey,

And I was like a Jaguar waiting in the cut,
True enough the truck they got in said Uber,
The critical mistake was killing my big brother
OG's,
Then having the nerve to speak on it,
Like that shit wouldn't make it from 3rd base,
Let me tell you this,
Keep your dirt to yourself,
No matter where you think you're at,
There's always ears of the enemy near,
That's why these 3 junkie ass jerks went from that Uber,
To this trunk,
I off'd one of them already,
Just to show the other two niggas,
Play time was over,
We had a barn in the country,
Just for this type shit,
I called the Big Homie,
I told him to meet expeditiously,
Of course he did,
When I pulled up,
I saw him pulling in,
He asked me what's up,

I looked at him, and grinned,
T, I love you bro,
Guess what I have in the trunk,
He gave me a look,
I knew the look meant,
Nigga it's 3 in the morning,
So I spilled the tea,
As I explained,
I saw the love and murder in his eyes,
You could see the burning rage,
The rage wasn't only seen by me,
The horror in the eyes of the two niggas left alive,
Was apparent,
They both began pleading,
Asking for an explanation,
Big Homie didn't even give them the satisfaction,
To my surprise,
He didn't do anything that I could've imagined,
This was real life,
Big Homie played it that way,
I swear the nigga was here before,
He never played this game like it was game,
Pop…..pop,

That was that,
He looked at me,
He smirked,
Then said thank you,
I love you O,
Dump the trash and link up with me,
Just like that, No torture,
No talking,
No explanation,
The only conversation held,
Was with me,
Now you ask me,
That was some real gangsta shit,
Not some Hollywood bullshit,
But some true to life shit,
So I dumped them niggas in the pig pen,
They'd be erased,
Only seen again as shit,
Digested by the pigs and probably eaten again,
Nasty creatures,
But who am I to judge them,
I ate bacon, pepperonis, and sausage,
So I was no better than them,
Regardless,
My point is this,

These hoe ass niggas got what they got,
I was happy to serve Wilbur and his crew,
Every piece of these bitches,
Tomorrow was today at this point,
Those lil blocks these hoes had needed to be covered,
So I gave their workers an option,
They all fell in line,
They knew what the fuck was going on,
It's not if they had an option,
Not unless they wanted to join their bosses,
A fate they could only guess and ponder,
Clarity was in the fact that I extended the invitation,
My name had weight because of my reputation,
To see me personally,
Was the threat in itself,
And within the threat you knew,
If you got down with us,
It was til death,
At least in the sense keeping your business to yourself,
I wrapped all that,
I'd like to believe I did my job to the T,
It hadn't even been a full 24hrs,

And there was no more static,
It was like I was meant for this shit,
As if I was on automatic,
I knew I needed to collect some paperwork,
The load would land in a few days,
I needed to make sure my lil bro was good,
He was my first priority,
Then came my lil love Yaya,
My lil Puerto Rican love,
She'd been here from day one,
She helped me raise my lil brother,
While still maintaining school,
She was older than me,
But I was way beyond the
numbers that represented me,
If you're from the struggle,
You hear me quite clearly,
Ya was in her last year of college,
For now she was getting her associates degree,
In business,
Bae was a genius in my eyes,
So I followed her,
The same way she followed me,
We rocked like that,
I even stayed solid,

Even when I could've fucked off,
I chose not to violate,
I wanted to be more than I'd seen,
I wasn't downing anyone,
No, not at all,
If I wanted a Queen,
Then I couldn't act as a prince,
And I saw the struggles of Kings,
Who would lose it all,
Because of their failure to tame their dicks,
We all had our own paths,
Even at 18 I understood this,
I wasn't perfect at everything,
But I understood,
It was because I had never allowed myself
to or even gave hoes any attention,
I felt like the way you respected home,
Was the way respect would be given to it,
And that's how shit went,
It was that,
Of maybe the fact that Yaya,
Had 2 under her feet herself,
Bitches may be thirsty,
But they weren't parched enough to die
for some dick,
That's why I fucked with bae,

That's why she was my fucking Queen!

Golden GoodNights

I walked into the crib,
And everything was off,
Including Teresa's clothes,
On my love for life,
Bae was a goddess,
How could I cheat,
Why would I,
My Granny told me,
And it was now clear,
Cheating was like Pandora's Box,
Once you opened it,
You would have to fight to close it,
The illusion it creates,
The fake sense of comfort you feel,
Is all manipulation,
You can't even understand,
Why you keep doing the things you continue doing,
Life continues to happen,

Everything you think you are,
Resembles nothing that you've become,
You're in hell,
But you think it's heaven,
You're not loving anyone,
When you think you're giving your all,
The reality is you're giving no one anything,
Granny was right,
I could see it so clearly,
I needed to get out of this game,
At 19 I needed to retire,
Not halfway,
But all the way,
Niggas ended up dead trying
to straddle the fence,
I saw it happen,
More than once,
You have to be a demon in this game,
It's a place where love gets you killed,
Trusting anyone was costly,
Even when it came to family,
I watched YGs kill their OGs
Seen sons kill their fathers,

Best friends go to war,
Over bitches and money,
Life in this game was no place for a family,
It was no place to even be a husband,
You couldn't win that way,
There's was no true power gained,
Just unneeded attention,
Happiness was the foundation
That built jealousy,
And jealousy was house,
That housed hate,
You're family would be a target,
A weakness,
A way to cut you deeply,
This game leads to less than,
And the goddess in my bed,
Laying here, making my mouth water,
Unknowingly being eye fucked,
Cranked up my imagination,
It was Really working ,
Devilishly,
It was creating,
I wanted to give her my best,

Starting with the way I was
about to devour her pussy,
But that would come after I took my time,
Kissing, and licking,
Twirling, and flicking,
Then stiffening my tongue,
Circling her asshole,
Before I began plowing my tongue inside her,
Again I say,
My mind was creating,
My manhood had created an imprint,
One that couldn't be hidden by jogging pants,
But I wasn't even attempting,
She rolled over on her stomach,
And her towel get caught underneath her,
That ass was exposed,
It felt like I was being teased,
She looked at me and smiled,
Then seductively Teresa asked,
" Bae, what are you thinking about? ",
Staring at my manhood,
Giggling sweetly,

Then tooting her ass up,
And spreading her cheeks,
I felt so thirsty,
So in need,
Of a satisfaction,
A fulfillment,
Only she could complete,
I wasn't wasting any more time,
I stuck my tongue in her pussy first,
Then french kissed her clit,
While my nose teased the hole
I would taste next,
I replaced my mouth,
With moist fingertips,
Gently massaging her erect clit,
Her moans motivated me,
As I ran my up and down her ass,
Kissing her cheeks,
Then sucking them,
Living a hickey on her left cheek,
Her back dipped deeper,
Convulsing as she released her nectar,
I wasn't going to waste a drop,

But that game plan,
Led to her cumming,
Again and again,
Unable to even talk,
So she didn't even attempt,
I wasn't going to stop,
I wasn't full just yet,
She was no longer holding her cheeks apart,
So I gladly squeezed them both,
I happily began fucking her ass with my tongue,
Pushing it deeply,
Trying to find more tongue to go deeper,
Without taking my tongue out,
Easily lifting her frame up,
And guiding her upon my face,
I was now on my back,
Enjoying the sight of watching her ass bouncing,
Turned on more and more,
Each time her cheeks smacked my face,
From reverse cowgirl,
She turned her body 180 degrees,

Now looking into my eyes,
As she stuffed my mouth with pussy,
Gyrating her hips,
In circles, zigzags,
Then attempting to smother me,
Teresa caressed her on breast,
Massaging her nipples,
And again I felt her body quake,
Then go limp as she exploded,
She was panting,
Breathing as if she'd ran a marathon,
I attempted to raise up,
Thinking she needed an intermission,
But I was wrong,
Bae had her mission of intentions,
Stripping away my jogging pants,
Then licking the tip of my dick,
Slowly tracing her tongue down to my nuts,
Sloppily she began to suck them,
Only taking them out her mouth,
To attempt to eat my piece,
Gagging and slobbering,
Purposefully creating a mess,

Knowing she had my toes curling,
Relentlessly slurping and stroking,
She felt me swelling up,
She could feel the veins in my manhood tighten,
I grabbed the back of her neck,
And fucked her mouth like it was her pussy,
I was about to cum,
Naw, I was about to bust,
Then bae pulled up,
The look on my face spoke clearly,
But before the words could form in my mouth,
Bae was sitting on it,
29 seconds later,
I was unloading,
Teresa wasn't done though,
She kept my dick standing tall,
Slowly bouncing and gripping my pole,
Bae erased the opportunity for us to hold a conversation,
After that 2nd nut,
A quick shower,

And nut 3,
I was snoring,
Slobbering,
Oblivious to everything,
I guess I loss that round,
Or did I win that round,
Shid if that losing,
I want to lose every day,
For the rest of my life.

A Golden Vision

I woke up to the phone ringing,
Everything was off,
I was in darkness,
Darkness created my surroundings,
I saw nothing,
Nothing but the phone,
It's light illuminated the bed,
Only the bed,
Beyond it's ringing illumination,
I saw nothing,
Again the phone rang,
Wait,
"Where is Teresa?",
My mind came up blank,
As my eyes fell upon her empty pillow,
Just an imprint,
Evidence of where she once lay her head,
Again the phone began ringing,
I retrieved it,
Then I noticed,
It read unknown in the display,
A number I usually never answered,
The next time it rang,

It said Teresa,
Then I quickly answered,
" Bae!?" ,
I spoke with hopes of hearing her voice,
Those hopes would diminish,
As I listened to the replying voice,
It wasn't Teresa,
It was,
" Mr. Byrd, this is Amanda, we've been trying desperately to reach you,
Miss Cartwright has been in a terrible accident! "
I wanted to speak,
But my voice wouldn't mouth words,
I wanted to move,
But my body wouldn't respond,
Tears begin to fill my eyes,
I had no control of them as they fell,
I was trapped within this misery,
The voice of Amanda drifted away,
Slowly things started changing,
Then in an instant they transitioned,
The phone became red roses,

Their hue brought upon the awareness
of death,
The bed became a chair,
One that was filled with familiar faces,
The darkness became a casket,
Teresa's temple was lifeless,
It was cold,
So cold my body trembled,
I tried screaming,
My eyes filled with tears,
Tears that began flooding the room,
I soon found myself unable to breathe,
I wanted to grab for her,
Yet I was still unable to move,
My body, yes, my body,
I could now see myself,
Unable to move,
But Teresa was laying with me,
She was wrapped within my right arm,
My breathing,
I began to choke,
Then I began to move,
I came back into my body,

I screamed,
As sweat dripped from my forehead,
And tears dropped from my eyes,
Just then I noticed,
I felt her warmth,
Her breast pressed into my back,
Her face was against my shoulder blade,
Her wrapped as far as they could reach around my abdomen,
She spoke softly,
Her vibes eased my soul,
" Bae, I got you! ",
I knew she meant it,
I didn't even respond,
I just turned around,
I grabbed her gently,
Then hugged her,
I hugged as if I had lost her,
I cried on her shoulder,
She cried with me,
We cried together,
She could always feel my pain,
Finally she found the words,

"What's wrong?",
I responded,
" I love you! ",
I didn't need an interpreter,
I had full understanding,
Understanding from my perception,
Death wasn't the only way to lose her,
There are so many more painful realities,
I needed to protect her,
I needed to encourage her,
Love her,
Be her strength,
Not her weakness,
It was time to end my nightmares,
I was now able to see the beauty within our dreams,
I had to try harder,
Today was the beginning,
I couldn't think of what could possible go wrong,
I had to plan for it still,
Yet planning for,
Didn't mean I was expecting to fail,

Either way I wanted to be with my Queen,
Whether as a rich man,
Or as a poor man,
Teresa's love made me wealthy,
She was more important,
She was much more valuable,
A dollar couldn't never come close
to her worth,
I promised myself I would treat her right,
Starting by straightening things within
myself,
I didn't need to tell her,
I needed to show her,
Dreams were worth having,
Worth believing,
Worth fighting for,
I promised myself I'd love this woman,
I had no idea,
Nor did I care about the obstacles,
I just knew 100%,
I had to fight these demons,
If I wanted to keep this angel in my world!

Golden Light Reveals the Secrets of the Dark

As soon as the Sun told the moon
it was time to go,
I was putting things together,
I was serious about closing this chapter,
I couldn't stop trappin,
But I had to,
Lil O been bossed up,
I had no worries about that
I knew bro was ready,
But even so,
I needed to have my ducks in
a row,
I had to prepare for the next step,
I needed to find my purpose,
But first,
I needed to cut ties with these anchors,
I didn't want to play the game
like a fuck nigga,
I needed them to know,
It was over,
The shit was done,

I was with Teresa,
On that note,
I needed to come clean with her first,
She deserved the truth,
But would the truth hurt worse,
It was my demon,
It was my guilt,
But her homegirl,
Wouldn't have the satisfaction of
Teresa's love,
That shit had to die,
Unfortunately I needed to create the why,
But why would that why be,
Just as I thought it,
Just as I began to devise a plan,
I got a text,
Then at least 5 more,
Then 5 more behind that,
There were screenshots,
Screenshots of every word between us,
I was too late,
Stacey dirty ass beat me to the punch,
I couldn't do shit,

My mind raced,
My heart skipped beats,
My body was stuck,
I was living within my dream,
It was happening,
Like de ja vu,
The events flashed through my mind,
I was getting what I deserved,
Anger ignited in my soul,
Murder exploded in my mind,
Then I felt it,
Maturity coming over me,
The realization of it all,
I couldn't kill her,
This wasn't on her,
It was on me,
She knew what she was doing,
She gave no fuck either,
In that moment,
More than any other,
I felt myself changing,
I knew I would lose her,
It was too much,

It was far too shady,
I did would I did,
I made my bed,
So I had to lay in it,
I didn't respond,
I didn't lie,
I didn't run,
Well not too far,
I needed time,
I wanted to tell her I was sorry,
But not over the phone,
I wanted to beg her not to leave,
But I knew I didn't deserve her,
So I drove,
I drove, and I drove, and I drove,
I didn't know where I was going,
I just wasn't ready to face it,
Teresa had been calling nonstop,
I decided to just let the bitch ring,
For two hours bae was relentless,
What she didn't know,
Was the pressure of it all,
On the last ring,

Of the last call,
I smashed my phone,
Then I threw that bitch,
It was floating,
Like a dead body,
It and all of its pieces,
The lake would devour it eventually,
I didn't need to watch the phone sink,
I was procrastinating,
Dragging my feet,
I knew what I was about to face,
I knew what this shit was going to take,
See I'm only 19,
But I know people,
I've studied people,
And I understand them,
I understand fairness too,
Teresa had the right to leave,
She had the right to say fuck me,
She had the right to do whatever she wanted,
And I had to be man enough to take it,
I needed to be man enough to face it,

So I headed home,
I didn't know if she would be there,
I wanted her to be,
I wanted to start over,
I wanted to be free of the guilt,
But I didn't want to lose her,
Not her,
Not the only woman I've ever loved,
Not the only woman to ever love me,
The only woman outside of family,
Outside of my mother,
And she's been gone 6 years,
Over the past 6 years,
Teresa has been my rock,
She's been my friend,
More than anything else,
How could I do this to her,
Why would I,
If the shoe was on the other foot,
I don't know how I would've took it,
Or if I could even taken it,
Bottom line,
She deserved better,

She deserves better,
And I have to give her what
she deserves,
Even if it means I'll be broken,
Even if it means what we have is
done forever,
I'll still be her friend,
Because I love her more than life itself,
So it's understood,
It's until death,
And everything going on now,
Was on me,
I could only point the finger at myself,
I needed no help,
My mind raced recklessly as I
pulled up to the house,
Her car was gone,
As I expected,
I had taken too long,
Now I had to sit in this house alone,
Our home,
I walked in,
And music was playing,

I didn't know the song,
But I listened to the lyrics,
It was a man bashing song,
You know that type,
Ones that make relationships
hard to hold together,
Then I saw a note on the kitchen counter,
Next to headless teddy bear,
The head, and stuffing everywhere,
I read it reluctantly,
I knew the words would be hateful,
I knew she would cut me deep,
But I faced it,
And it read,
" I trusted you,
I truly believed,
This line you've crossed,
Kills me,
It feels like I'm suffocating,
But I don't think you care,
I don't think you love anything,
So I'll raise my child alone,
My child won't be your next victim,

And I won't be your fool,
Not anymore,
I can no longer do it,
I've been faithful,
I've been honest,
I've always been there for you,
Always there to love you,
But you've never loved me,
Because you don't even love yourself,
Don't come looking for me,
Call that bitch Stacey,
Maybe y'all will be happy together,
Because you and I are done,
No matter how much I love you,
I'm worth so much more than that,
I deserve someone's best,
Something I assume,
Was too much for you to handle.
Love,
 Teresa,"
Damn,
That's all I can say,
Tears fell relentlessly,

She was really gone,
She was really fed up,
I was alone,
But I wouldn't just give up,
I couldn't,
I had to fight for her love,
True enough,
I didn't deserve her now,
But I wasn't going to allow now,
To become an ongoing scene,
My actions would change it all,
Even if she wasn't here,
I needed to make changes,
I had child coming,
I couldn't allow myself to be my parents,
I wouldn't allow my child,
To feel the pain I had felt,
I had to grow up,
I needed to be something greater,
And I would be,
I just had to do it,
But do what next,
I had no idea,

It was ok,
I knew whatever I did,
I would succeed at it,
Not for me,
But for my family,
I was going to marry Teresa,
But first,
I needed to become a King,
No first,
I needed to become a grown man!

GOLDEN INSTINCTS

I found my focus,
I was motivated,
I was ready,
I had my head in the game,
I was thinking,
But never before had I
thought the things I was now
beginning to think,
It had been 3 weeks,
She still hadn't returned one call,
So I stopped even trying,
There weren't anymore tears
for me to cry,
I started to study myself,
I needed to know my gift,
I needed to understand my
greater attributes,
So I could apply them to
getting money,
I knew I enjoyed business,
So I knew whatever it was I did,
I would be great in that aspect,

I understood the difference
between a job and a career,
I was know worker bee,
I wasn't a fuckin Queen either,
I was a man,
I was a boss,
I was a owner,
While I was handling my business,
I was thinking,
What was Teresa doing,
Why didn't I chase her,
I should've went home,
I should've answered the phone,
I was heading to O crib,
Each reup to me,
Was like a countdown,
I needed to be better,
I just didn't know how,
Maybe I wasn't focused,
I wasn't focused at all,
Anytime she invaded my thoughts,
My thinking became an endless ocean,
One I couldn't swim in,

One I couldn't escape either,
Like a Chinese yo-yo,
It squeezed my heart tighter and tighter,
The more I struggled with the pain,
What could I do,
I needed to find my bae,
I pulled up on O,
He was pacing back and forth,
I could damn near see smoke,
I could tell he was angry,
It wasn't difficult to see that
something was wrong,
So I hopped out the whip calm,
I asked him, "what's going on?",
He answered," the blocks been hot as fuck!",
"We took losses out East and out North!",
"How much O?", I asked,
"175k got took!",
My head was spinning now,
"How the fuck that happen?",
I was passed pissed,
This shit had me passed a buck,
He answered,"somebody's snitching!"

I asked immediately,"who!!??",
O, looked at me with a look,
I understood clearly,
It was time to set some mouse traps,
Starting with these niggas,
The ones closest to me,
Not O,
But his underlings,
I'd allow da young bull to handle his wax,
Still I'd do my own digging,
See what I could come up with,
2 heads are great than one,
This wasn't a competition,
It was a mission,
One that needed to be handled,
Immediately,
How much did they know,
How long had this rat been around,
This made me lock in,
I regained clarity within now,
Thoughts of Teresa were smothered,
I had to keep my focus,
I was playing a high stakes game,

Look at the fuckin loss I just took,
O, saw my frustrations,
He looked me in the eye,
Confidently,
I felt his words to the heart,
"I'ma kill the nigga!".
I knew he meant it,
I didn't respond,
I just tilted my head,
Then answered my own questions,
In my head,
I broke it all down,
I thought about who had access,
I thought about who had the nuts,
Even when talking about a rat,
You immediately think,
Coward, spineless, fuck nigga,
All those things,
Which are true,
But what can't be overlooked,
Is them telling,
Then continuing to come around,
Knowing any day could be

their execution,
You tell me I'm wrong,
That takes nuts,
Nuts that would be cut the fuck off,
But still,
I knew it wouldn't be easily seen,
This person wouldn't arrogant,
Cocky, real grimy,
Maybe even have several bodies,
It didn't matter,
The nigga had to go,
I told O to make an example,
Teach these niggas bout playin,
In fact I'll be there myself,
We dapped up,
I headed to my whip,
As soon I opened my car door,
I heard a car accelerate,
I didn't even turn my head to look,
I had a pole on the seat,
I just upped that bitch,
I pointed were my hearing took me,
I didn't even think it was the dicks,

I knew it wasn't,
The niggas thought they caught me slippin,
Any thought the driver had was gone,
I saw exactly what he was thinking,
It hit the dashboard,
The windshield and on his partners,
I hit them first,
They didn't even get a shot off,
The Altima they were in,
Swerved then hit a pole,
It was two other niggas in the car,
I slowly approached,
Lil O was on my heels,
We were on some military shit,
TTG,
TRAINED TO GO,
Murder without understanding,
I didn't want to kill both of them,
O shot one of them in the face,
Right below his right eye,
There was no chance he would survive,
He slumped immediately,
And immediately we heard another

voice yell,
I'll tell you everything,
Please just don't kill me ,
The voice had no bass,
As if it was from a child,
Even worse,
It was a child,
And he was scared to death,
Before we could even ask,
He told us who sent him,
I turned my head ,
I heard the round go off,
I felt no remorse,
O felt none either,
This was at his crib,
That nigga had no understanding,
Although he maintained his composure,
He knew he had to move,
Living this close to the hood,
Had left him vulnerable,
We knew who to hit,
O hollered at his wifey,

I got more magazines,
And made some calls,
Niggas was bout to feel me,
The young nigga told us
Old Head Bobby sent him,
A nigga we had no ties with,
I didn't even think of the bitch
as competition,
We knew where to find him,
I saw him going to his car,
Just like me,
The biggest difference was,
He wasn't me,
And I wasn't some scared
lil boy,
I was a veteran,
A killer, that had all intentions
of killing him,
So I parked solo,
The guys knew their missions,
This wasn't our first rodeo,
We all had our own mission,
O was in charge of the guys,

On some black ops shit,
Him and 3 others,
We didn't need an army,
Just enough to cover all corners,
Which they did,
Silently,
The same way I was approaching
this dumb ass nigga,
He was calling someone,
Over and over,
I assumed he was calling the
3 niggas we murked,
As soon as he thought to look in
his side view mirror,
It was too late,
He had an automatic shotgun on his face,
He didn't move,
He just said, "so they missed?",
I didn't respond,
So he continued with what he
had to say,
"It's Lil Keith, he paid for your hit!",
2 birds 1 stone,

I blew all his facial features off his face,
This was a closed casket event,
12 bodies,
None of them was from our team,
We were in and out,
5 minutes tops,
We now had a birds eye view of the situation,
It would have to wait,
15 bodies in less than 24 hours,
On the way back,
I got a call I wasn't expecting,
It was Teresa,
I didn't even hesitate,
I quickly answered,
She was in a panic,
Asking me if I was ok,
I knew that meant O's wifey had made the call,
I was good with that,
I needed to hear Teresa's voice,
She asked," Are you ok?!",
I answered sincerely, "I love you!",

She responded, "I love you too!",
I asked for her to meet me at the crib,
She agreed,
O looked at me smiling,
Then asked, "So you still getting out the game?",
I looked out the window,
I thought for a second,
Then replied, "Teresa's my greatest concern!",
I was focused,
I was determined,
We had to chill for a few weeks,
Let the oven do what it would,
The streets would be cooking,
I wasn't about to my team in the way,
So the shop was closed,
I needed to think,
You couldn't just kill a CI,
You had to plan everything,
I left it in O's hands,
I knew he wanted the pleasure,
I was headed to the crib,

My next step meant everything!

A Golden Acceptance

Love's Unconditional Understanding

When I pulled up to the house,
My mind had taken me to the
hitter that was a kid,
I thought of my own,
Then I thought of myself,
That night my parents were killed,
I remembered the terror,
I felt so alone,
I was so scared,
I was hidden in a spot,
That allowed me to view it all,
And I did,
Still I didn't make a sound,
I don't even remember breathing,
I just remember waking up,
My grandma and my uncle were crying,
Holding me,
Broken,
But grateful I was alive,
I never told anyone but Teresa,

She had been there for me,
I had to be here for her,
I needed to be a father to our seed,
I needed to be her husband,
Her mate,
Her partner,
Outside of this trap of the soul,
Money had its purpose,
Still would it be worth it,
If I was taken away,
Whether by the grave,
Or the penitentiary,
It would create the same void,
A hole of emptiness,
Filled with resentment,
Filled hatred,
Darkness,
Anything that didn't equal love,
I wouldn't become that story,
I was better than that,
I loved her more than that,
It was time to empty my clip,
Let go of all the secrets between us,

I walked in the crib,
She was sitting in the kitchen,
Reading Lost & Found THE AWAKENING,
A book by Stephen Talley,
A book she had been told was amazing,
Tears were falling from her eyes as she read,
I knew whatever she was reading,
Had to be something that resonated with us,
As I entered the kitchen,
She looked up,
Folded the corner of the page,
Then closed the book,
I approached her lovingly,
Gently removing the tears that
continued to fall with my index finger,
Then with my lips,
As I kissed her cheek,
I hugged her tight,
She hugged me back tighter,
I leaned back,
I attempted to apologize,
She placed a finger on my lips

before my lips could even part,
She buried her face into my chest,
She cried deeply,
She'd missed me as much as I missed her,
I won't lie,
I could care less what you think,
We cried together,
We needed one another,
I knew this moment meant we'd be
together forever,
I knew it's what I wanted,
I felt it was what she wanted,
I took a deep breath,
I was prepared to take the step,
This was my soulmate,
My twin flame,
My Queen,
The other half that made me breathe,
I appreciated life because she was in it,
I wasn't broken because of my past,
I was dirty because of my own decisions,
I cheated because I wanted to,
My choices were based upon me,

I was thinking about myself,
Only about myself,
I was selfish,
That shit had to end,
Self meant us,
Self meant our family,
I wasn't going to hurt this woman,
Never again,
The trust that I had broken,
I would rebuild,
I wouldn't speak on it,
I was going to let my actions give my intentions clarity,
I wasn't going to say,
What I knew was expected,
I placed the blessing upon myself,
I say a blessing,
Because it was a chance I didn't deserve,
I should've been 100 from the beginning,
Not 97, 98, or 99,
Anything less than 100 wasn't 100,
Period,
Exclamation point,

I was a boss,
I was a king,
I was a man,
My decisions are what gave my
claims weight,
To claim to be something you're not,
Is fraudulent,
It was foogazy,
It was fake,
None of what I felt,
None of what I believed,
None of that shit described me,
I wouldn't allow it to either,
Being flaw at anything,
Meant I was flaw at everything,
Like bread,
If any of it was molded,
You would throw it away,
In your mind all of it was molded,
If it was true or not,
You really didn't know,
In this case I do know,
I wasn't going to be anything

less than a buck,
Teresa lifted her head up,
Her eyes were red,
Slightly puffy,
I could see the pain she had gone through,
The disbelief,
The betrayal,
The courage she was showing,
Her being here was gangsta,
Her being here was powerful,
She loved me,
So much so ahe believed in me,
I kissed her,
Before her lips parted to speak,
Reciprocating the way she had treated me,
Not wanting the moment to be lost,
Enjoying the happiness and fulfillment,
I needed her here,
Not in the house,
But in my life,
I kissed her deep,
Our tongues clashed gracefully,
As we began to part,

She gently sucked my bottom lip,
Pecked me,
Then she began to undress,
I stepped back and admired her beauty,
My tongue and dick jumped,
Both were ready,
She looked at me and giggled,
Then said, "I know you ready to kiss some ass?!!",
I smirked, licked my lips and answered,
"I'm going to kiss it, lick it, and tongue fuck it!",
"Don't play!", I said smiling,
I lifted her little frame up,
Sat her on the counter and kissed her again,
Then I attacked her neck,
But I wouldn't leave her marked up,
She hated it,
And I would respect it,
So I moved to her left breast,
Devouring it whole,
While caressing her right nipple,
Gently running my finger tips

over it,
While I treated her left nipple like her clit,
She was going crazy,
Her body vibed vigorously,
I could feel the warmth of her pussy
on my stomach,
I could feel her wetness,
But I wouldn't disrespect her right breast,
I would deprive an inch of her,
So I blessed both the same way,
Before turning her over,
Yeah, it was going down,
Fuck the bed,
Fuck the couch,
Right here on the island in the kitchen,
What better place to be fed,
She tooted that ass up,
Happily without any shame,
I decided to drive her ass crazy,
Make her cum right now,
I wouldn't even touch her,
The anticipation was going to fuck her up,
I attempted to play my game,

Teresa wasn't having that shit,
Her little hand reached back,
She palmed the back of my head,
And fucked my face,
I tightened my tongue,
To dip in,
Widening it once in,
Twirling it,
Flicking it,
Licking up and down her pretty ass,
She couldn't hold my head any longer,
She decided to spread her cheeks instead,
She moaned and lightly giggled,
I love when she did that shit,
It made me go even harder,
It made my dick harder than trig,
Her pussy was leaking on my chin,
She was exploding,
I wasn't going to let her waste it on my beard,
I wanted her juices on my tongue,
So I put my whole tongue in her pussy,
My bottom lip massaged her clit,

It was so erect,
My nose teased her asshole,
She was shaking and trembling,
Her body was going crazy,
My face was covered in her juices,
I touched her abdomen,
She had started to show,
Bae was filled with my baby,
I started sucking her clit,
Rotating it with my tongue,
While applying pressure,
She never stopped shaking,
She was trying to run,
This wasn't like the first or second nut,
This one,
Had the feeling of 3 or 4,
She couldn't take it anymore,
I wasn't ready to let go,
But I did,
She turned over on her back,
Trying to catch her breath,
I blew on her pussy,
She couldn't even handle that,

Teresa moaned,
"Baeeeeeeee !!!! Pleeeeeaaassse !!!!",
I laughed,
She laughed,
We laughed as I stepped outta my pants and shoes at the same time,
She was sweating,
Lightly on her forehead,
I couldn't even tell if I was or not,
If I was,
It was mixed with her juices,
She raised up,
Kiss my lips,
Then licked hers,
Kissed me again then sucked my tongue,
She used her big toes to push my boxer down,
She wanted the dick inside her,
It wanted to be in the same place she wanted it,
It needed no guidance,
I slide straight into her,
I've never been the type to think there was

a difference between fucking and making love,
Today I felt the difference,
It didn't matter where it was,
It didn't matter what position,
What mattered was her,
It was the feeling,
I felt as if I was in her soul,
It felt as if she was in mine,
I didn't want to rush to a nut,
I wanted every second of this moment to last,
It seemed as if I hit the right spot every time,
I was deep in her,
Then I'd slowly pull out,
Sucking her titties in rhythm with my stroke,
We came in sync,
As my manhood grew,
Bigger and bigger,
My veins could even be felt,
Her kegel muscles tighten,

As we both exploded,
Both sweating,
Both realizing this was different,
She pulled me to her,
Looked me in my eyes and said,
" I love you Terrence, don't ever cross me again!"
Then kissed me before my lips could part,
Letting me know,
Nothing else needed to be said!

The Golden Crown Of A Queen

We were moving forward,
Shit was really better than it's ever been,
I was free from all my lies,
All but one,
One that wasn't truly a lie,
It was more so lack of effort,
This game was all I've known,
Leaving it,
Seemed so hard,
I guess that's why it's called a trap,
Because mentally you're locked in,
You lose all sight of reality,
You're even depleted spiritually,
Love is so hard to have,
When everyday could be your last,
With that mentality,
How could you think beyond the moment,
When any moment could be your last,
I often heard my Granny tell me,

Conversation is vital,
To have success within any relationship,
In any way,
You have to know how to hold one,
It was a necessity to know how to talk and listen,
A fool filled with arrogance,
Is not a leader,
They were followers of themselves,
If your voice is all you hear,
You value no one else,
That alone eradicates the identity of a leader,
A leader followed,
Those they had placed in places for that reason,
A leader surrounded themselves with leaders,
It created a balance of power,
The head of the snake wouldn't exist,
The tyrant type,
Those filled with arrogance,
The narcissistic fool,

Trusted no one,
 Do so made them weak,
Failure would soon find them,
It would always be close,
It would always be near,
So I talked to Teresa,
A King and Queen depend on each other,
It's the balance of their thinking,
That created the power to run a kingdom,
I didn't want to hide my struggles,
My weaknesses could be her strengths,
I was right too,
I didn't even have to start the conversation,
She initiated it,
She was truly an empath,
Able to feel my vibes before I even spoke,
She asked, " You want to talk about it?" ,
I spoke to her honestly,
I let her know I was struggling with letting the game go,
She listened,
Not once did she attempt to interrupt,
I told her I was afraid,

I was scared to let her and our seed live a day without me,
I asked her how would I be something else,
When this was all I thought I'd ever be,
I kept the problems of the rat to myself,
I tried hard to keep the streets and home separate,
My uncle gave me that jewel,
Home hadn't been everything I'd wanted,
Still I took a lot from it,
Jewels were plentiful,
Knowledge was spilled everyday,
All but the knowledge I needed now,
No one ever taught me how to escape,
As Teresa began to talk,
I listened attentively,
I shut out all other thoughts,
She spoke without bias,
My Queen was so fucking understanding,
She started by saying,
"It's all about you,
It's all about what you think is important,
Money is straight,

So what is the real problem?",
None of this was meant to be answered,
All of it was rhetorical,
So I didn't speak,
I allowed Teresa to continue,
She continued by saying,
" If you apply your best efforts,
I know you can do anything,
It only seems hard now,
Because it's new,
It's the fear of change,
You're not simple minded,
Nor are you unable to be greater,
I apologize for placing you under so much pressure,
This isn't all your fault,
I'm with you through whatever,
I'm afraid too,
Remember,
My life hasn't been as hard as yours,
But bae,
We were raised in the same hell,
Our traumas are different,

So I understand,
The things you've been through,
Is the reason I'm afraid,
Your past is why change is so difficult,
It's why you have no problem taking another life away,
Because those meaningful to you,
Were taken from you,
You only spent 13 years with your parents,
That alone,
Is something most could never shake,
Of course your Granny loves you,
Still she could never be your mother,
The love is different,
Still, she gave you all she could,
Believe me,
I know, in truth I could never understand,
I have never faced those obstacles,
I never want our child to either,
I don't want to be a widow,
A single mother bringing our child
to visit you like a zoo animal,
I need you,

We need you,
That's why I asked you to change,
Because I've seen so many die,
I watched too many mothers cry,
I've seen the broken souls,
You're so much more than this,
I believe in you,
I believe in us,
I know you have the ability to be great at anything,
You've taught yourself,
Study without be lectured by a teacher,
Think beyond what you know,
The same way you have always done,
You weren't always a boss,
You had to become one,
You put yourself in this position,
Nobody gave this to you, but you,
Our livelihood was created from your abilities to elevate your thinking,
You know how to adapt,
Now that you've been a boss,
You can't become content,

Bosses can get fired,
They're just as expendable as a soldier,
Like a rook to a king,
This is our board,
It's time we took control of everything!",
Teresa was blowing my fucking mind,
She was really giving me everything I needed,
She said one last thing that resonated so deeply,
It was as if my mind was fertile soil,
She was planting the seed of change,
It's was up to me to water it,
It was up to me to allow it to sprout,
Teresa maintained the same compassion,
As she looked into my eyes,
She said it so clear,
As if she had thought out all these things for months,
She said, "Bae, your time as boss has to end,
It's time you became and the owner,
The owner of everything,
Starting with yourself,

You're not alone,
We will do all this together,
The burden of our future,
Isn't a burden at all,
It's a gift, it's a pleasure,
One I am grateful of,
I look forward to each moment,
It doesn't matter if we're rich,
It doesn't matter if we're poor,
We're forever going to be wealthy,
Because we will always have
each other!" ,
Yeah, I know right,
Teresa was something special,
She was dope,
For real,
She was that forever type,
Unique in every way,
I felt her in my soul,
I knew I would always love her,
I knew it was time to take the next step,
My birthday was in a couple weeks,
I decided my birthday wouldn't be about me,

It would be the day,
I asked Teresa to marry me,
I'd waited long enough,
She reached out and grabbed me,
Interrupting my thoughts,
She whispered in my ear,
" I love you!",
I whispered in hers,
" Until death……",
She cut me off,
Then ended it with,
" Finds out that it could never do us part!"
Teresa was the dopest woman I'd ever met,
She was the beat of my heart!

A Golden Hit
NO FACE, NO CASE

Too much time had gone by,
Still, I respected T's mind,
He had never let us down before,
I knew what was at stake,
Wouldn't allow him to do so now,
One thing I had always had problems with,
Was patience,
Big homie always told me,
He always reminded me,
"O, the most valuable characteristic
is patience, but know the difference,
Between patience and procrastination!",
As time went along,
I was starting to understand,
It was crazy,
Patience was the key to clarity between,the two,
As I sat thinking,
In the basement of my new spot,
I was still not sleeping well,

And wouldn't sleep well,
Not until we handled this little wax,
These niggas could hurt my family,
They could've taken things I could never replace,
The guilt of the what if,
Was driving me crazy,
I knew what came with this life,
I knew,
Yet, I couldn't see myself doing shit but this,
While in that thought,
My phone rang,
It was T,
He told me to link up,
And be quiet when I come in,
Teresa's knocked out,
I knew what that meant,
It was time to put in work,
He didn't have to say shit else,
I knew where to meet,
I knew how to come,
Be quiet when you come in,

Meant, twist the suppressors on,
I knew this nigga was on the job,
Even with his wifey coming back home,
Like I said,
"Too much was at stake to play!",
I knew he was feeling the same way,
I met T at his crib,
We left our phones intentionally,
We needed no distractions,
We hopped in a low low,
An old bucket with light tints,
Some kind of Chevy something,
It was all white,
No hubcaps,
A real POS,
T lived out in the woods,
He had parked the car at an
abandoned shack,
We walked like two miles to get to it,
I understood the precautions,
It's one thing to off a nigga,
It's another thing when you off a nigga
in bed with the dicks,

We weren't dummies,
Never would be,
Never had been,
T had set the nigga Keith up,
He knew like I knew,
That nigga loved to trick,
So he had sent two bitches his way,
All three of them were about to get lost,
All loose ends had to go,
At the moment they were at a hotel,
One on the outskirts,
That nigga Keith had a bitch,
I wonder how she'd feel,
To know he got smoked,
Because he was tricking on some bitches,
Funny to think,
It wasn't my problem though,
I got comfortable in the backseat,
Made sure AR15 was ready,
Then we waited,
A few hours later,
We saw all three hop in Keith's Camry,
We knew where they were going,

So we laid back a block,
We saw the nigga get on the EWay,
This was when we would strike,
T hit it,
The little raggedy piece of shit was getting up,
I pulled my mask down,
Got the street sweeper ready,
Anything this bitch touched was about to get shredded,
Keith dumbass was slipping,
Freaking and geeking,
Dumbass nigga wasn't even paying attention,
I was in the backseat,
On the driver side,
As T pulled up right next to the nigga,
We rolled steady with the nigga,
I could see him clearly,
The light skin bitch in the backseat could feel it,
She kept looking at us,
These light tints were like 5% on this part of the slab,

Keith was getting sucked up by the other bitch,
I hit the button to let my window down,
When it was 3 quarters of the way,
I aimed at that nigga top,
I knew he was dead,
I watched his brains come out of his skull,
Still I hit that bitch with all 30 rounds,
Before that nigga car swerved,
Then somersaulted over the guardrail,
Wasn't nothing but a cliff on the other side,
This wasn't a movie though,
We heard no explosion,
It didn't matter,
We both knew everyone was dead,
That was no longer the mission,
It was time to get rid of everything,
So we did,
As planned 6 miles up,
Right off the exit,
Outside the city limits,
Was a shop,
Our shop,

For destroying shit,
Just like this,
We had a crew that asked no questions,
The same crew that was on the last mission,
We watched as they dismantled,
Then they melted everything including our clothes,
Nothing was left,
Nothing,
No ties could be traced back to shit,
We got dropped off in the woods,
Made the two mile hike,
Then we were back at T's crib,
As expected,
As planned
We both had numerous missed calls,
No tower could tie us to a damn thing,
It was a flawless victory,
Yea I know,
I know what you're thinking,
We didn't have to kill the two bitches,
In truth,
We didn't,

Yea I may have done what I did,
But dirty shit,
Happens to dirty people,
Nothing but a triple cross could beat
a double cross,
We weren't going for that shit,
Not yesterday, not today, and not tomorrow,
This game is a cold mothafucka,
You had to stay one step ahead,
Obviously none of them got the memo,
Neither of them bitches knew either of us,
T didn't have to explain,
I knew he did what he had to do,
So I didn't ask,
I didn't return any calls either,
T and I didn't even talk,
He dipped off to lay up with Teresa,
I would go home in the morning,
I knew Bae was worried,
Still, the plan was that we were sleeping,
No calls were answered for that reason,
No calls could be made either,
I wouldn't have to explain shit,

She knew the game,
She knew if I wasn't answering,
It was for a reason,
Her and my lil bro were good,
And the nigga that committed treason,
Was dead,
I said I would kill that nigga,
And I did,
I felt at peace,
I felt as if my family was safe,
So I fell asleep,
Peacefully,
For the first time in over 30 days!

Golden Beginnings and Painful Endings

I can't lie to you,
Getting myself prepared
for this next step,
Was something I was excited about,
I was ready for whatever,
We had shutdown the block
for 2 weeks now,
Niggas was starving,
But that wasn't my problem,
We said it was a drought,
And since we said that,
That's what it was,
The dicks were doing what they do,
We were just paying attention
to them,
The way they pay attention to us,
It was time to move on for me,
And time for Lil O to set up shop
outside of this trap,

Everything was about evolving,
Today I turned 20,
Yea just a dub,
And what I'd learned in 20 years,
Was crystal clear,
Nothing can stay the same,
You're either elevating,
Or you're falling behind,
Doing nothing,
Equaled gaining nothing,
Even if you decided to sit in the crib,
Open a fuckin book,
Watch some documentaries,
Do something to gain,
Rather than doing shit that drained you of life,
I was never the type to party,
Never the type to spend time with niggas
I knew nothing about,
I had many demons,
Had done too many things,
To ever feel like I was comfortable enough,
To be on some let's kick and depend on them

to make sure we guarded,
Fuck that,
Not in my city,
Not with Teresa, O, and his Mrs,
Hell naw,
Tricks were for kids,
And I had done enough of that on the bitches,
I didn't need a rug to sweep shit under,
And I didn't need a helmet,
Because I wasn't no fucking crash dummy,
So for my birthday,
I had only one agenda,
To make it something for Teresa to remember,
I wanted her to have all the shine,
Believe me,
She deserved every ray of light,
Especially tonight,
On my night,
I had the dopest little set up planned,
And it would only be the family,
Including our blood too,

Teresa, wasn't an orphan like me,
I could only imagine how this would go,
I know for years,
Her people tried to tell her I was no good,
All of them but her OG,
Mrs. Lacey loved me for who I was,
In truth she was a gangsta at heart,
Not because she sold drugs,
Not because she bodied some niggas,
None of that shit that means nothing,
She was a gangsta because of
the way she raised her daughter,
Never allowing her to be green,
Or allowing her to wonder about nothing,
She kept it 1k with her at all times,
The same way she was with Teresa,
She was with me,
At all times,
I promised her to take care of her baby,
She responded so real,
It made me feel small,
Made me take the shit 100 times more
serious,

She told me not to make stupid promises,
Nobody could protect anybody in this world,
Not alone,
We all had to protect each other,
That's why Teresa was so surgical with all weaponry,
Not because of me,
But because of her OG,
I just kept her on that shit,
Honestly though,
She kept me on mine,
My phone rang,
Breaking me from my thoughts,
It was O letting me know everythang was a go,
It was 5:03,
We needed to be at the Hilton by 7,
We were meeting up in a completely different city,
Providing the transportation for the whole situation,
I didn't want any excuse from anybody,
And didn't get an excuse from any one,

We linked up at the Hilton, in Parksville,
It was like an hour away,
I had the ring on deck,
It was yellow gold,
Because that's what bae loved to wear,
But it was flooded in diamonds,
Bugs Bunny would've had a field day,
Then he would've got his ass smoked,
Yea, I know,
That's some cold shit,
But I am who I am,
And just because I'm evolving,
Doesn't mean you want get yo shit punctuated,
Teresa looked at me smiling,
Happier than I was for my birthday,
I understood why she felt that way,
She laid down every night,
Praying our feet touched before
the sun came up,
So she was happy to be with me,
20 years old and going,
I was 5 years ahead my time,

I was retiring before I even turned 25,
And I was on some real boss shit,
I had enough money to do whatever with,
But that shit would have to wait,
Mrs. Lacey had prepared all the food,
She had a catering service,
And offered to be the service,
Because she knew how special the
night was for us,
Plus she knew I loved her chicken,
Mac n cheese and mashed potatoes,
Not to mention this cake she
just sat in front of me and Bae,
She looked at me and smiled,
Grabbed my right hand,
And squeezed it,
Then told me Happy 20th rotation,
Kissed my forehead,
Then told us both she loved us,
I ate the smallest piece of cake,
On God a young nigga was nervous,
I didn't want to get the Bg's,
And fart as I dropped to one knee,

So I held off,
It was go time,
Mrs. Lacey set it off,
She asked everyone to get in the picture,
Then told everyone to fall back,
Everyone but me and Teresa,
We posed then I acted like I was tying my shoe,
Mrs. Lacey asked Teresa,
"What is Terence doing?",
As she looked down,
We met eye to eye,
I didn't even get to ask anything,
Teresa was already crying,
Her eyes were overflowing,
She couldn't stop them if she wanted to,
Her tears created my tears,
And I wasn't ashamed of none of them,
I gathered the words,
"Teresa, will you marry me?",
She couldn't even get the words out,
She just nodded her head,
I slid the ring on her finger,

The room erupted with nothing but
positive vibes,
Everyone had tears in their eyes,
And was smiling uncontrollably,
Teresa pulled me up,
Hugged me,
Kissed me,
Then hugged me again,
She was so happy,
So filled with all the things I wanted her to
be,
She deserved this moment,
I felt so weightless,
Yet so full,
I didn't care about anything
else going on in life,
I was completely engulfed in this moment,
Teresa turned to the family,
Stuck her below thirty two finger out,
And screamed,
"I'm gettttttttiiinnngggggg
maaaarrrrrriiiieeeeddd!",
Everyone rushed in to congratulate us,

But no one reached us before her mother,
She whispered to us both,
"I always knew the two of you,
Would never letting each other go!",
Her face was coated in tears as well,
We both told her we loved her,
Both of us thanked her,
Then she thanked us,
Before we could even ask,
She answered,
"This is better than a Lifetime movie!",
We all laughed,
My Granny and Uncle,
Both were still crying,
She hugged me like she wouldn't see me again,
That took me for a ride,
A quick vision flashed through my mind,
I saw my parents,
I saw their eyes,
So I hugged my granny tighter,
My uncle grabbed my shoulder,
He mouthed silently, "I'm proud of you.",

Everyone was in high spirits,
Just as I started to think
about my parents again,
Lil O grabbed me,
We shook up,
But he can sense something was up,
He asked me if I was straight,
I answered honestly,
"I think something is wrong with my
Granny!",
He asked me why,
I told him straight up,
Something felt funny,
O kept it a buck,
Whatever it may be,
It's not up to us,
I acknowledged his point,
My homie looked at me,
Then told me,
"Out of all the Boss shit you've ever done,
this is by far
the most Big Boss shit you've ever done!",

I knew how he felt about treating your
Queen like a Queen,
So that meant a lot to me,
I respected it,
Because I knew how he treated his love,
I can't lie to you,
I'd be a flaw ass nigga if I did,
The emotions from the moment drained us,
After everyone left,
Teresa and I made our way to our suite,
We didn't fuck or nothing,
And it didn't make us a fucking difference,
We showered,
And passed out,
We didn't cut on the tv,
We didn't plug in our phones,
We were too exhausted,
But the knock at the door,
At 4 am,
Could've only meant one thing,
Something wasn't straight,
It was O,
He was sweating,

Tears mixed with his sweat,
He told me my Granny had a massive heart attack,
I didn't even ask,
I already knew the answer,
That was life though,
My baby was on the way,
But not before I lost Granny,
The day after I proposed,
The morning after the day,
I turned 20!

A Golden Cry

LEARNING TO GRIEVE

Somehow I already knew,
Somehow I had already accepted
what O was telling me,
Teresa was in the doorway of the
bedroom fully dressed,
She hugged me,
She asked me am I ok,
All of it was so comforting,
So naturally,
She grabbed her keys and headed
for the door,
She said she'd be at the hospital,
Get myself together,
She'd have her mother meet her there,
She hugged her O on the way out,
Asked him was he straight,
He just nodded,
Still crying silently,
My Granny meant a lot to him,
Just like she did to me,
We both were orphans,
She'd been there for us both,

Never treating O like he wasn't family,
She treated him like he was my brother,
She created the expectation that made our bond,
"Family was who you didn't choose to have,
Yet you have,
That is what's special about it!",
"So never say you don't have nothing,
because it's a lie, you'll always have family!"
That's what my granny use to say,
Some of the realest shit I've heard to this day,
I live by that shit too,
Only difference I made to it was this,
Understand who your family is,
I understood quite clearly,
I understood why O, felt like he did,
Teresa said told me she loved me,
I gave her the same energy back,
Still trying to put together the next steps,
No tears came,
Not even one,
Yet I still felt the pain,

I felt like I'd always felt,
Like anything I ever loved was always taken,
It's why I never did anything but fake it,
I was scared of moments like this,
Teresa was the only girl I ever loved,
I was only 20 and I had to learn to understand,
Nothing but love could ever be kept,
Unless I held on to the pain,
It had drove me insane,
For years I never knew how to grieve,
I cried deep in the shower,
Even though I had come to terms with the shock,
I still felt the pain of the loss,
I wouldn't carry this weight,
So I cried until the water began to get cold,
One walked out the room O,
had gathered himself,
I myself,
Felt as if all the tears I had to cry,
Had been cried,
I felt free of the grief,

There was no pain to hide,
No burdens to carry,
I let go of what I couldn't keep,
I held on to what would never leave,
We headed out,
Not even speaking,
Yet silently understanding,
Then just like that,
We were at the hospital,
Of all the family we had,
The one's present,
Were the ones I knew would be,
What I didn't know,
Was that I was about to get a call from the plug sayin we needed to meet,
The money was straight,
Even though we had locked down the streets,
Maybe he'd heard about the rat,
Or seen for himself,
Not shit was going on,
I can't say,
Nor do I give a fuck,

I never take shit I can't pay for,
Even if he think he fronting me,
I send the paper as soon as I see
what ain't been paid for,
I've never been a fool,
Or under the rule of someone else
because I owed them,
The respect was established,
Because I've never folded,
I've always stayed solid,
Always, even when I had pennies,
I was never raised to hate,
Or wait on the next man,
I was taught to listen,
But to always think for myself,
Teresa looked at me,
As I hung up the phone,
She told me she loved me,
Be careful, and she'd make sure
everything was taken care of,
I hugged everyone,
I thanked them for being there,
As I turned around,

They rushed in,
Told us to put our hands up and lay down,
We were being arrested for the murders of the rat and them two bitches,
I expected this shit last week,
These hoe ass dicks hadn't gotten desperate,
They were bringing us in for one reason,
To make us tell on ourselves,
I'd understand their thinking if I was weak,
I'd understand if O, was any different than me,
They just blew their whole case,
They were going to try to press,
Thinking we'd slip because we were depressed,
There was no depression,
Even it was,
You can't slip,
If you keep your mouth shut!

Golden Code
Keep your mouth closed

We never got a chance to speak,
Nor did O and I need it,
Nothing needed to be said,
Nothing would be said,
Nothing but let me see my lawyer,
We knew they didn't have shit,
They knew they didn't have shit,
So all they could attempt to do,
Was play us against each other,
They knew they were on a limited amount of time,
No bond would even be needed,
The whole case had been botched,
You could see the frustration on these bitches faces,
The sleepless nights,
The stress of not having a way in,
They wanted us so bad,
You could see how much they hated us,
Wishing they could torture us,
Wanted to chop off our fingers,

Drowning us in water until we couldn't
take it,
Problem is,
They couldn't ,
Even larger problem is,
We were being held on suspicions of
absolutely nothing,
Our alibis were sealed tight,
And that's exactly why those two hoes,
Had to go that night,
What do I look like,
Who the fuck do they think I am,
Do you really think I'd put my life,
In the hands of two hoes,
Are you fucking slow,
Well maybe you are,
But clearly as you can see,
I am not,
This bullshit they just pulled,
Was all but enough,
As my lawyer busted in,
Breaking me away from hearing any further
manipulation,

Everything that comes out they hoes
mouths is bullshit,
Talking about they just want to help me,
If I could just help them,
I just smirked,
Almost letting out a laugh,
Ready to tell them hoes,
To kiss my ass,
But I didn't,
They'd get no emotional shit from me,
No conversation,
None, not even my name,
I know my rights,
They even tell you niggas,
You have the right to remain silent,
Somehow you bitches still open your mouths,
The foogazi type anyway,
Off brand ass niggas,
Deserve exactly what the fuck they get,
I don't talk about what I've done,
I don't feel big,
Because I am big,
I know who the fuck I am,

I was made this way,
I wake up like this everyday,
I'm solid, will be solid, and
that's not to be questioned,
Anybody can shoot a gun,
Most people will take another's life
to protect their own,
But how many will really keep their mouths
shut,
Stand on what they say,
Regardless of if it means they gotta
go lay it down,
This life doesn't force you to be in it,
No matter what cards you've been dealt,
You always have a choice,
Play your hand out,
Or fold your hand and take another route,
I chose to play,
It's the game of life,
If it's life that's the game,
I choose to play mine at high stakes,
I don't like McDonald's,
I want a fucking steak,

I don't want a Nissan,
I want a fucking Audi or Merecedes,
Struggling to pay rent,
That ain't even in my DNA,
My O.G.'s won't be rolling over in
their graves because of me,
My name means something,
My family safety and well being,
Is partially on my shoulders,
Even though I put it all on my back,
I won't belittle my misses,
She's everything that describes,
My better half,
Things I can't see,
Things I can't understand,
She is all the things I will ever need,
Everything I could ever want,
As they uncuffed me,
And I begin to walk out,
The black officer,
The nigga looked like he just came out the stove,
Black mafuckas mumbled under his breath,

"Does your fiancé know she'll be raising her child as a widow?",
On my love for life,
I made a mental note,
I was going to blow up that nigga house,
I smirked,
Then I responded,
Noticing his wedding ring,
"You and your family take care.",
No malice,
No emotions,
Bitch nigga came out the chair,
Hands around my throat,
Attempting to end me right there,
That's all I needed,
It's all it took,
Before we left the station,
I'd be filing an attempted murder charge on this bitch,
Not for him to go to jail ,
Naw,
This gives me the right to kill him,
Naw all I need was to create the situation,

If we crossed paths by coincidence,
And he attempted to do say shit,
I'd have my man's with the license to carry,
Pop his top like a soda,
I wouldn't press the issue for now though,
I filed the report,
Then saw O,
He looked at me and grinned,
We didn't have to say shit,
Not now,
Not at our cribs,
Or on the phone at any point,
We had already been planning to go,
This was confirmation,
We had less time than we thought,
If the little letters can't do it,
It's only so long before the big ones catch our drift,
We thought they already had,
I still think they did,
That's we were moving a fucking crumb,
Would you think I was lying,
If I told you,

This had all been a part of the plan,
I know it's hard for you to understand,
But I promise,
I swear,
I studied these mufuckas like they study us,
That's how I know these bitches are desperate,
You have to study the opposition,
You have to understand them,
So you can be steps ahead of them,
Regardless of the rat,
He never saw me doing shit,
Never heard me speaking on shit,
O and I talked,
That where it ended,
Naw I did have my go to squad,
But that was a hold different beast,
These niggas had proven themselves,
They were cut from the same fabrics as me,
O and I found ourselves ducked off,
We went to the spa,
A place a wire couldn't be worn,
A place we never went,

Surveillance wouldn't have a leg up,
That's what we would be do,
Anytime we would meet,
If not at the house,
It would be somewhere we'd never met before,
A place off the wall,
A place that know person would think we would go,
Still we would speak how we spoke,
In our code only we know,
We chopped it up,
Got the point quickly,
I needed to get to Teresa,
Shid O was going to the same place with me,
His wifey was waiting like mine,
We still had a funeral to arrange,
But we had many more things to plan,
It was time to leave,
It was time to evolve!

A Golden Partnership

Learning to Follow As A Leader

It wasn't an option at this point,
Not in my eyes,
Not for me,
I knew like we all knew,
Staying any longer than the time
it takes to move,
Was out of the question,
I wouldn't tell a soul,
Neither would O,
Those that needed to know,
Already knew,
I hadn't even had the opportunity to
call the plug back,
My phone was with Teresa,
She wouldn't answer it,
She'd probably even cut it off,
Which made me think,
I'd never felt so focused,
I was able to think,
And not about dumb shit,
It felt good to be free of that destructive

bondage,
I planned to never go back to that,
I wanted more from life,
I wanted more for my wife,
More for my child,
More for myself,
My family deserved to be free,
I couldn't allow them to go through my bullshit,
Just because I was afraid to be better,
This game could do a lot of things,
80% of those things were pointless,
90% of them could hurt others,
100% of them were dangerous,
Only 1% was worth it,
There had to be another way,
I knew there was,
It was time to take this shit further,
And I knew just who to invest in,
The Uber pulled up to my spot,
I had a plan,
A simple plan,
Teresa was the key to it all,

Naw, I wasn't going to put her to work,
I was going to let her guide the boat,
I had my ears wide open,
I had plenty to learn,
I needed her,
But before I even got a chance to speak,
The moment the front door opened,
Teresa was on me,
She hugged me tight,
Then kissed me slow,
I kissed her back,
Deeply,
Lovingly,
The energy naturally just flowed,
She knew my body,
She knew my soul,
Her love was golden,
She was so beautiful,
The baby bump was showing,
Her face had filled out,
Bae was thicker than ever,
With everything going on,
All the ups and downs we'd faced in

72 hours,
Had bae unbelievably horny,
I could tell from the way her eyes touched me,
My soul felt secure,
My heart felt cherished,
My mind felt grateful,
And together the credited confidence,
We both knew,
This love was forever,
Her lips gently pressed my jugular,
After her tongue had tasted my skin,
My vibed uncontrollably,
As my Queen undressed me,
While letting her robe fall,
She grabbed my manhood,
She stroked it,
Then firmly squeezed it,
My veins had expanded,
My girth demanded her grip to loosen,
She had guided my energy to her level,
My mouth watered,
My eyes closed,

I envisioned her beautiful smile,
My dick stretched even further,
Bae gently pushed me down into the chair
in the living room,
Kissed me again,
Then dropped to her knees,
She licked the tip of my erection,
From the tip,
To my balls,
Then back to the tip,
She was treating me like ice cream,
But I wasn't melting,
I wasn't about to bust any time
soon either,
I wanted to lick every inch of her frame,
But she wasn't trying to let me get turn,
She wasn't trying to let me think,
I attempted to touch her,
Without breaking her rhythm,
She pushed my hands back to the cushion,
Then lightly moaned as she caressed my
balls with left hand,
She was applying vice grip type pressure,

I heard myself moan in satisfaction,
She knew just what to do,
She knew just how to do it,
My body was reacting to her touch,
Not just her mouth,
Not just her tongue,
Not just the way she moaned as she attempted
to take more of my soul,
Her fingertips made my body involuntarily go crazy as fuck,
She loved me,
I knew that, and had always known that,
Then I relaxed,
I allowed myself to enjoy it,
Here I was thinking about getting my turn,
Which I still wanted,
But she had the floor,
She had the wheel,
She was enjoying the taste of me,
She was enjoying drive my body crazy,
She was enjoying having me in this moment,
We hadn't even had a chance to do anything

since our engagement,
Or should I say my birthday,
Or should I say the day my Granny died,
Or should I say the day the police came and got me,
We had been hit so many ways,
Before we could even breathe,
So I took a breath,
This was step one,
I allowed myself to let go,
It wasn't a competition,
I didn't have to be in control,
I trusted her guidance,
I trusted her intent,
She licked my balls,
Then begin sucking them,
She spit on them,
Sloppily massaging them with her tongue,
I needed to touch her,
I wanted to taste her,
I could smell her aroma,
It made me want her so much more,
I couldn't take it,

I attempted again to touch her,
This time I got no resistance,
We truly were in sync,
I squeezed her titty lightly,
Not knowing if I'd make milk come out
I squeezed them,
She looked in my eyes and grinned,
I lifted her up,
So I could kiss her again,
Goodness she sexy,
Nothing about Bae was average,
Nothing about my Queen was ordinary,
I was about to eat her ass right now,
God I was addicted to her everything,
I told her to toot that ass up,
Again, no resistance,
She even helped the situation,
Spreading her ass cheeks then clapping them together,
I was bout to eat that ass forever,
At least that's how it made me feel,
She was so fucking sexy,
I smiled as I noticed her engagement ring,

I wasted no more thoughts,
I kissed her pussy lips,
Her clit was already exposed,
Her pussy was already soaking wet,
I licked the juices from her pussy lips,
Then I sucked and tongue kissed her throbbing clit,
The tables had turned,
Now she was the one lost in thoughts
OH MY GOD,
Unable to do anything but moan,
I was lost in the moment,
I was cherishing everything about it,
And had barely even gotten started,
I knew what she was anticipating,
I knew she loved it,
So I gave her what she wanted,
Honestly we both did,
She tasted good where ever my tongue landed,
And it landed right between her ass cheeks,
Her body shook with excitement,
I licked up and down,

Front to back,
Then I circled her tight lil asshole,
And slid my tongue as deep as it would go,
I bounced her ass on my face,
Making them smack me,
As I enjoyed every drop of her juices,
Her moans made me not want to stop,
My dick was hard as life,
I wanted it to be,
The same place she did,
She moaned it softly,
"Baby put it in",
She was beyond wet,
She was soaking wet,
I was so ready to feel it,
As soon as I dipped my dick in,
She came again,
Her pussy grabbed my tighter,
She was really about to put me out of commission,
So I hit the gas,
I beat the pussy up,
I knew I was going to make it,

I lasted for about 8minutes,
And we came at the same time,
I have no lies to tell,
And I don't feel embarrassed,
Not a little bit,
Not at all,
We were both beyond satisfied,
We could get another round later on,
Right now we just needed to shower,
Then lay down and regroup in the morning,
We hadn't been home in 2 days,
And within 30,
This would no longer even be our home,
We had a lot of things to handle,
So we would rest,
And shift into gear,
The moment our eyelids spread apart!

Golden Words Upon Paper

Just like that,
We were bustin a move,
Teresa had the ball rollin,
You know what's even more solid,
She had that bitch rollin without me,
Before I could even say shit,
When I woke up at 7,
She already had shit packed,
She was rooted in front of her laptop
like a plant,
She already had 3 properties in line,
Squared off,
With only her finances at stake,
Teresa was on some overdrive shit,
Not in a bad way though,
Queens are Queens shit like this,
I didn't even want to wait to have a wedding,
So I told her,
Well, at I tried to,
She faded me,
She told me to get focused,
All that for the public shit,
Can be done,
When we do it in the public,

You've been my King,
Do you need the world's approval to treat me like your Queen,
All I could do,
Was what she said without speaking,
Do you wonder why I love her,
I don't either,
I know why,
She just keeps adding reasons,
I said, " I love yo momma!",
She giggled, and blew me a kiss,
Still typing,
With her eyes locked in,
I had to let her be,
So I decided to link up with O,
We needed to have a sit down with the socket,
There wasn't much to do,
But we needed to get it done,
We were supposed to meet anyway,
Things had now changed,
I would be respectful; of course,
I'd listen, pay attention, and answer with a

few words,
Unless more words were a need,
As we got to the meet spot,
Everything was how it always is,
Nothing seemed off beat,
As of yet, or as we sat down,
Lonni spoke defiantly,
"Everything good? How's your family? What do they know?",
I knew he already knew I knew, he knew,
I wasn't fucked up about telling him shit,
I'm solid, I didn't have shit to hide,
People that lack morals, or self worth,
Wouldn't be sitting here,
Again, he already knows what's up,
But for his comfort,
I ran down the list,
From the beginning, middle, to the fucking end,
Which is now,
He just nodded,
As my story hit every key note,
That sang the song of truth,

It moved our conversation along,
He asked what I planned to do,
Then asked how things were going with
Teresa's new venture,
Again subtly letting me know,
His eyes are literally everywhere,
He told us of his real estate experience
across the country,
He caught eye contact with me,
Then grant me his best wishes,
We knew that meant he'd be in touch,
We set things up,
To set things up,
While we continued to figure things out,
We had the plugs blessings,
I ain't the type to half step,
I wanted my feet out the water,
That's what he gave me,
But he wouldn't let me go completely,
Things had to still operate through my voice,
He trusted O to be what he was;
Nothing more,
Which is all I could expect,

Until O proved himself,
No different than me,
His moves carried the weight of our lives,
And I trusted him completely,
Or I wouldn't even put him in this position,
Shid, I didn't even put him in this one,
O been a Boss,
I've never been his leader,
We're brothers, we depended on each other,
We're playing this game to win,
So we kept our moves to our chest,
Of course I knew Lonni was aware of
Teresa's
real estate business,
It's what I needed the nigga to see,
But we had other shit steering in the point,
We had some things of our own we were
working on,
O's family was already moved out of sight,
Unknown to the public,
And even family,
There was one more thing,
Only I knew about,

Until now, as I walked in the house,
Teresa was sitting on the couching reading,
Tears just falling,
And I didn't have to ask,
I knew why she was in tears,
She asked me, "how long!",
I responded, "Since you found out you're pregnant!",
She responded through real sobs,
Terrence, this is some of the most beautiful poetry I've ever read in my life,
I just nodded my head,
Then I answered, "I didn't find it Bae, it found me!",
She reached for me,
And I hugged her little pregnant frame tight,
I told her,
Y'all brought this out of me,
She ask me to read it to her,
So I did,
"It doesn't matter if you fail the first time,
In fact,

Let's just skip to try 1 million,
This is what the love for a dream looks like,
An endless amount of effort,
A painfully optimistic mindset,
A relentlessly ambitious heart,
That will only accept success,
Failures are embraced,
This is self motivation,
When you reach your destination,
You'll be mentally prepared to maintain
your success,
As you continued beyond your vision,
The picture will continue to expand,
As you realize every step taken has been
a goal accomplished,
Expanding simultaneously with the
growth of what you believe,
Strengthening the connection between
the heart and the mind,
Your sacrifice for your success,
Is the epitome of love,
Love designs a greater picture,
You reached for a 50 inch flat screen,

Love gave you an IMAX theater!".
She kissed me and softly whispered,
You're an amazing man,
I know you'll be an amazing Father,
There's nothing you can't do,
I know, because I believe in you,
With all of my heart!

My Golden Queen
Teresa

It was the day of the funeral,
Everyone was in sync,
Trying to help each of us stay a float,
We were all smiling, laughing, and being that genuine vibe,
Appreciating one another's company,
Acknowledging the reality of losing a loved one
is a large pill to swallow,
It takes the unity of family to heal the wound,
We all feel the presence of pain,
We won't all deal with it the same,
But when we're together,
We can all uplift one another,
While we have one another,
A blink is all that separates any of us from death,
Knowing that,
Is why I stand by who I love,
He's made many mistakes,
But it's not that upon to judge his struggles,
I see the effort,
We always want results,

But we're so reluctant to take the steps to
make it there with them,
It's not about what I want,
And it's not right to put pressure on anyone
to be anything,
So I've stood where I stand,
Holding his hand,
While we stare at his grandmother's
beautiful temple,
No longer filled with life,
Just an empty shell,
What we won't ever be,
I'm filled with our love,
A part of me feels like the soul of his
Grandmother landed within me,
She was so tough,
She'd seen so many things,
And survived it, to live to be 87,
Her Indigenous American skin was beautiful,
Only light wrinkles existed around her eyes,
87 was a full life,
I wiped T's tears,
As he attempted not to cry,

He always felt the need to be strong,
So I allowed him,
Until I knew he needed to breath,
Life always gives you signals,
If you're being attentive,
See while you're thinking about you,
You're partner could be falling apart,
Your truth will show,
With time,
And his truth is showing,
It's shining,
And I believe it always will,
I love who I love,
Who I love believes in me wholeheartedly,
I've been through so much throughout my life,
My struggles have never been judged,
They've only been assisted, and uplifted,
If I've ever needed anything,
I could depend on him,
Do you know what that feels like,
To have someone that's your own,
You don't have to wonder,

Because You know,
Find the reason you believe,
Hold on to it,
Until they take it away,
He hasn't ,
And I truly believe in my heart,
Death won't even steal our love,
I was thinking while holding his hand,
Right here, right now,
In this very moment,
Filled with this beautiful seed of light,
We watched them close her casket,
Carry the casket out,
Drop the casket down into the ground,
Shovel the dirt on top,
Everyone leave,
Then there was only us,
In our home,
We laid in the dark,
He fell asleep,
Then I fell into my mind,
I wouldn't let him down,
I had my plan together,

I'd be stacking as long as I'd been working,
I had $86,000, of my own money,
Tucked away,
Hidden from T or anyone else,
Even myself,
I wasn't thinking about a rainy day,
I was thinking about being what he needed me to be,
Without him having to tell me,
I needed to stay on my pace,
In my space,
Focused on my priorities,
Creating goals for our family,
It's my job to create, nurture, and literally be his rock,
Not just in emergency situations,
But also in times of needing comfort,
Times of needing guidance,
Times of needing a smile,
Times like these,
When I needed to be on my shit,
And I was,
I told you about the 86k,

I also have another 13k invested,
That started from 500 little dollars,
I've learned to play the stocks well,
Real estate was also something I'd already studied,
It was something I had an interest in,
Then there was nursing,
In just a few more months,
Like 14 more months,
I'd be a LPN,
I don't think that will be my field interest,
But I'd finish,
Because that's me,
The ball was rolling,
I'd have our new house set up,
Our new beginning would be amazing,
I believed in us,
How can a King fail,
If his Queen plays her part,
Exerts her power accordingly,
Their greatness depends on them,
The both of them, together,
I believe in life,

Because I believe in love,
I believe in us,
Because we've survived the storms,
And we're ready for what's to come,
I believe enough for us both,
But I don't need to,
Because his beliefs in us,
Are just as massive,
We both know without any doubts,
We were each other's reason,
I believed we both believed the bundle of joy
in my belly was our purpose,
Life had blessed us,
After everything we'd faced,
The most important part is that we survived,
We stayed together,
So we grew together,
We fought to become something greater,
We struggled,
But we never fell apart,
That's what makes it all worth it,
That's how I know,

And that's why I'm fearless,
Because he's without fear,
I trust him,
Those were my last thoughts,
As I crawled into bed,
My body was exhausted,
He opened his arms,
And I fell in,
Our heartbeats found each other's rhythm,
I was sleep before I could even become restless,
Life was a dream within a dream,
And I was grateful for every part of it.

A Golden Creation
MY SEED OF LIGHT

4 months had flown by quickly,
We were having a girl,
Marie would be here any day now,
I won't lie,
I'm scared, and I'm anxious,
But ready and excited,
I've never felt this way,
Not this way,
No! Never like this,
It almost feels as if we've already met,
Sounds crazy,
But I promise,
I feel her within me,
But not like her mother,
Lol, her mother,
My Teresa had gained 60lbs,
All while showing me,
The meaning of her crown,
I'm beyond amazed by this woman,
To do what she's done,
At the magnitude she's doing it at,
In this 4 month span,
Is beyond amazing,
In 120 days time,

Teresa had accumulated 600k,
Profit,
She started with her own money,
These were her moves,
She would discuss the situation,
We'd come up with a solution,
But she was handling everything,
The even crazier thing,
She did it without a dime of my money,
She was so fucking sexy,
I didn't invest in her brand,
She wouldn't allow it,
I didn't have to hold her hand,
She didn't depend on me,
Not for that,
She didn't need me,
Not for that,
She loved me,
That's the only reason I was in her life,
Because I was me,
I respected that,
She was ready to get this part done,

She couldn't wait to get back to her petite self,
She was looking forward to fucking myself like she was in a rodeo,
I had proven to her over and over again,
She was the most beautiful woman on Earth,
Honestly she is,
Fuck what you think,
Your thoughts mean zero to me,
Why would I listen to you,
About my Queen,
I trust her with my life,
Not you, you, or you,
Not any of you,
Just her,
And what has trusting her gotten us,
The same thing as her trusting me,
But even greater,
That's why she's my better whole,
I blow up the world for those I love,
Snatch your food out your fridge,
Kidnap your bitch,
Or I might just cut your dad's foot off,

For playing with anyone I love,
So don't fuck with my core unit,
Unless you don't care about life,
But anyway,
Life was moving, improving,
And I was enjoying every minute of it,
Lil O was doing his thing,
His lil unit was rocking,
O head was in the game,
O, still moved around like old times,
He was a grown man,
Able to make up his own mind,
Either way, I would be in his corner,
No static come from the case,
They never had shit,
Knowing that,
Is why O, still made our blocks
continue to be his own,
You could someone consider me ,
Retired,
But not really,
I still had to be the bridge between O, and
the connect,

Which didn't cause much of a rift,
Although it did piss O, off,
He wondered why Lonni, didn't trust him,
It was hard to explain,
People don't like change,
No matter what financial status,
I think those that are controlled by money,
Can never truly be trusted,
O, wasn't cut like that,
I vouched for that,
I would never question his motives,
I'll go slump the connect right now,
But I honestly wouldn't want to put my
family in the type of heat,
I trusted O,
Regardless of his frustrations,
I knew he knew the business,
He wouldn't throw this opportunity away,
He wasn't afraid of death,
But I told him,
I reminded him,
There are things much worse than death,
And more painful than torture of the body,

It's power is felt by the body,
It weakens the immune system,
Torture created by a broken heart,
Can be extremely destructive,
The loss of his brother or his wife,
Would destroy him,
Starting from the inside,
I reminded him of what he needed no reminder for,
But still,
The truth is they missed the first time,
How many times do they miss,
Exactly,
That's what I'm trying to plant in his heart,
If he put our families in that type of shit,
I'd always feel the need to burn him,
If he played me raw like that,
We'd body them niggas,
If the universe kept us alive,
He's blessed,
There's no need for me to calculate stress,
Expect failure,
Or manifest the shit by fearing it,

There was no need for fear,
That'd mean I was ungrateful,
And I'm not,
My mind is doing what it does,
So my heart had to step in,
Teresa's grind has been so relentless,
And I've been out the way,
I found something I love,
Something that feels so unlike any job, or hobby,
It felt like purpose,
It felt like life,
I'm good at a multitude of things,
I'm great at fewer things,
But only for the moment,
When you work at things,
Good becomes great,
But with writing,
It seemed as if I'm was starting from the point of great,
I had so much to talk about,
It just flowed with ease,
All the things I've gained,

And all the things I've gained from losing,
It seemed like everything I had faced,
Was for this,
So I could find this moment,
Then, within mid thought,
My phone chimed,
As if on que,
I got the call,
She was going into labor,
Her OG was cool, calm, and collective,
It was incredible to see her just be,
Meanwhile here I am,
Scared as fuck,
Driving, and attempting to pay attention,
But really not paying any,
Other than just straight forward,
But God was with me,
My Angels escorted me to the hospital,
I was out the car,
Up the elevator, and in a gown quickly,
Teresa was pacing her breathing,
Contracting, and squeezing my hand,
We both were sweating,

We both were squeezing each other's hand,
I looked at my mother in law,
She was just smiling,
Phone out; recording,
And I'm thinking I'm a gangsta,
Shid this woman was crazy,
And I was definitely making a mental note,
The I saw my baby,
Her hair, head, shoulders, and the rest,
Immediately it felt like we caught eye contact,
It was as if she came in this world looking for me,
And she found me,
But there was no cute smile after that,
Just a scream, followed by beautiful cries,
She was here,
Beautiful as ever,
Marie Monet was 9lbs 7oz,
and 22 inches long,
It felt like I was holding my mother, father, and granny,
All wrapped in one,

All I wanted, was all I had,
So many people like to create problems,
Play victim, then self destruct,
I'm not into being any of that bullshit,
Nothing in my life was broken,
If I was; I didn't give a fuck,
I wasn't in the game to lose,
I was a motherfuckin winner,
And there was only one way to win,
To create something greater,
For a greater reason than me,
It was all about us!

The first poem Teresa found:

Do you know what it feels like,
To be a young man,
To be a teenage boy,
Trying to become a man,
Without any guidance,
Just a mother trying,
Doing her best,
But she could never be a father,
That balance is something she just can't give,
All she can do,
Is everything she does,
Still, it's only 100% of half,
The other half is on the father,
It's his job to teach his son,
The part of his son that's him,
Once the balance is found
within understanding them,
He'll finally begin to grow,

The problem is the world he's growing in,
Is designed to break that balance,
Most times within this society,
Our homes are so broken,
We hardly find the words; I love you,
It's even rarer to find homes
that understand the expression,
For generations love has been
nothing but words spoken,
Treated like an obligation,
That they can't wait to rid themselves from,
Now think,
A boy growing into a man,
With only the side of him that's emotional
giving him guidance,
It's a major disadvantage,
When a man is meant to be logical,
How could he,
In a system that's stealing fathers,
Even as he becomes of age,
Having the pressure placed on him to be a man,

*Is as unfair as telling an infant,
To feed themselves!*

-T

Made in the USA
Monee, IL
22 September 2022

13574447R00115